S0-ARN-338

CHICKENS ON THE FARM/
POLLOS DE GRANJA

By Rose Carraway   Traducción al español: Eduardo Alamán

Gareth Stevens
Publishing

Please visit our website, www.garethstevens.com. For a free color catalog of all our high-quality books, call toll free 1-800-542-2595 or fax 1-877-542-2596.

Library of Congress Cataloging-in-Publication Data

Carraway, Rose.
[Chickens on the farm. English & Spanish]
Chickens on the farm = Pollos de granja / Rose Carraway.
    p. cm. — (Farm animals = Animales de granja)
Includes index.
ISBN 978-1-4339-7394-9 (library binding)
1. Chickens—Juvenile literature. I. Title. II. Title: Pollos de granja.
SF487.5.C3718 2013
636.5—dc23

2012008193

First Edition

Published in 2013 by
Gareth Stevens Publishing
111 East 14th Street, Suite 349
New York, NY 10003

Copyright © 2013 Gareth Stevens Publishing

Editor: Katie Kawa
Designer: Andrea Davison-Bartolotta
Spanish Translation: Eduardo Alamán

Photo credits: Cover, p. 1 Digital Vision/Thinkstock; p. 5 Menna/Shutterstock.com; pp. 7, 24 (feathers) Jaqueline Abromeit/Shutterstock.com; pp. 9, 24 (coop) Sean Malyon/Garden Picture Library/Getty Images; p. 11 Meister Photos/Shutterstock.com; p. 13 Sue McDonald/Shutterstock.com; p. 15 cynoclub/Shutterstock.com; pp. 17, 24 (nesting box) Jochem D. Wijnards/Photographer's Choice/Getty Images; p. 19 CGissemann/Shutterstock.com; p. 21 Guy J. Sagi/Shutterstock.com; p. 23 Steve Reed/Shutterstock.com.

Printed in the United States of America

CPSIA compliance information: Batch #CS12GS: For further information contact Gareth Stevens, New York, New York at 1-800-542-2595.

Contents

In the Coop 4

Roosters, Hens, and Eggs 10

Eating and Sleeping 20

Words to Know 24

Index 24

Contenido

En el gallinero 4

Gallos, gallinas y huevos 10

Comer y dormir 20

Palabras que debes saber 24

Índice 24

A chicken is
a kind of bird.

Un pollo es un tipo
de ave.

It has feathers.
These keep it warm
and dry.

Los pollos tienen
plumas. Las plumas los
mantienen calientes y
secos.

7

It lives in a special house. This is called a coop.

Los pollos viven en un lugar especial. A este lugar se le llama gallinero.

Male chickens are called roosters.

Los pollos machos se llaman gallos.

Female chickens are called hens.

- -

Las hembras se llaman gallinas.

13

Farmers get eggs
from hens.

Las gallinas ponen
huevos para el granjero.

A hen lays its eggs
in a nesting box.

Las gallinas ponen sus
huevos en un nido.

17

People use the eggs
for food.

Las personas usan estos
huevos como alimento.

Chickens eat many things. They like to eat bugs!

Las gallinas comen muchas cosas. ¡A las gallinas les gusta comer insectos!

21

Chickens sleep
in a group.
This is called roosting.

Los pollos duermen
en grupo.

Words to Know/
Palabras que debes saber

coop/
(el) gallinero

feathers/
(las) plumas

nesting box/
(el) nido

Index / Índice

coop/(el) gallinero 8

eggs/(los) huevos 14, 16, 18

hens/(las) gallinas 12, 14, 16

roosters/(los) gallos 10

24